based on a story by
Vladimir Grigorievich Suteev

DUCK, DUCK, GOOSE?

RETOLD AND ILLUSTRATED
BY KATYA ARNOLD

HOLIDAY HOUSE

NEW YORK

Goose looked just like every other goose, but she longed to be different. She was jealous of other kinds of birds, except for ducks. They looked too much like geese to interest her.

No one liked her, because she was always in a very bad mood.

One day Goose saw Swan. If I had a beautiful neck like that, thought Goose, everybody would want to be me.

"Swan, would you take my neck? I'll take yours," said Goose.

Swan thought Goose would be happier if she got what she wanted.

So they exchanged necks.

Pelican saw Goose and started to laugh. "What are you? You are not a goose and you are not a swan!"

Goose wanted to hiss at Pelican, but then she saw Pelican's beak. If only I had such an unusual beak, thought Goose.

"Pelican, would you take my beak? I'll take yours," said Goose.

Goose will look even funnier with my beak, thought Pelican. So they exchanged beaks.

Goose began to like swapping. She switched legs with Stork. "Stork, would you take my legs? I'll take yours," said Goose. "You will be a better swimmer. I will be the tallest bird around. Finally everyone will look up to me."

So they exchanged legs.

Crow has such shiny black wings, thought Goose. They will make me pretty.

"Crow, would you take my wings? I'll take yours," said Goose.

So they exchanged wings.

A kind Rooster offered Goose his red comb, plus his "Cock-a-doodle-doo." Goose accepted gladly.

Peacock is the most beautiful bird in the world because of his tail, Goose thought. I want it!

"Peacock, would you take my tail? I'll take yours," Goose suggested. "You can fly much better with my small tail."

So they exchanged their tails.

Now Goose did not look like any other bird.

"What kind of bird is that?" cried all the geese in surprise.

Goose proudly showed them her new neck, new beak, new legs, new comb, new wings, and beautiful new tail.

"I am a goose-a-doodle-doo!" crowed Goose. "I am the best!"

"Well, if you really are a goose, you can come with us," said the geese, although they didn't quite believe her.

They all went to the meadow to graze, but Goose could not eat even one piece of grass. Pelican's beak kept getting in her way.

So the geese all went to the pond and started to swim, but Goose could not join them. The stork's legs were too tall for the shallow water. "Wait-a-doodle-doo," she shouted, but they kept paddling away from her.

Suddenly Fox sprang from behind a tree. The geese took to the air. Goose tried to fly, but Crow's wings were too small.

She tried to run, but Peacock's tail got caught in a bush. She tried to swim again, but she could not. Fox grabbed Goose's lovely long neck and started to pull her away. "Help-a-doodle-doo," she cried.

The geese heard her cries and came to the rescue. They surrounded Fox and pecked him and bit him and pinched him from all sides until he let Goose go.

"Thank-you-a-doodle-doo!" said Goose. "Now I know what I need to do."

She found Swan and switched necks. She found Pelican and switched beaks. She gave back Stork's long legs. She returned his red comb and "Cock-a-doodle-doo" to the kind Rooster. Finally she switched tails with Peacock.

Crow begged to keep Goose's large wings, but Goose said she needed them back. Now she looked like every other goose. Only she was smarter, kinder, and happier.

And still prettier than a duck!

To my nephew Nikita, with love.
—K.A.

Author's Note

This story was inspired by an animated film called *Who is this Bird?*, which was directed by the great Russian director, Vladimir Grigorievich Suteev.

Suteev is often called the Disney of Russia. Born in 1903, he was a talented artist, screenwriter, and movie director. His sweet and funny films charmed a generation of Russian children. I hope that *Duck, Duck, Goose?* will carry on his tradition.

—K.A.

The artwork was prepared using a color baseplate of acrylic-painted collage and brilliant watercolor, with a separate overlay of black line.

Copyright © 1997 by Katya Arnold
All rights reserved
Printed in the United States of America
First Edition

Library of Congress Cataloging-in-Publication Data
Arnold, Katya.
    Duck, Duck, Goose? / retold and illustrated by Katya Arnold. —
1st ed.
        p.   cm.
    Summary: A goose who envies the attributes of other birds learns
to appreciate her own qualities.
    ISBN 0-8234-1296-2 (reinforced)
    [1. Geese—Fiction. 2. Birds—Fiction. 3. Happiness—Fiction.]
I. Title.
PZ7.A7356Du   1997   96-54856   CIP   AC
[E]—dc21